My ~~The~~
Book
With
No
Pictures

by B.J. Novak

and _____
your name here

Dial Books for Young Readers

This is a book with
no pictures.

It might seem _____
(ideas: boring, simple, wubby)
to have someone
read you a book with
no pictures.

It probably seems

_____.
(ideas: wonky, slipsloppy)

Except . . .

Here's the rule:
Everything the words say,
the person reading this
book *has to say*.

Which means I will

sound very _____.
(ideas: goofy, absurd, cool)

Especially if the words say . . .

BLORK.

B_____F.

(ideas: blarf, bruff, bafoof)

Wait—what?

That doesn't even
mean anything.

FL_____.

(ideas: floof, flork, fladdle)

FLuuRF.

Wait a second—what?!

This isn't the kind of book I wanted to read!

And I have to say every word the book says?

Uh-oh . . .

I am a _____
(ideas: crocodile, moobie-goobie)

from the mountains of

_____ .

(ideas: Bellyland, Sneezopolis)

Hey! I am not!

And now I am reading you this book with my

_____ mouth

(ideas: gumball, mighty)

in my

_____ voice.

(ideas: sandbox, pudding)

That's not true!

Oh, by the way,
I am also a _____
(ideas: purple, gigantic)

_____ •

(ideas: elephant, dragonfly)

Excuse me?

My favorite things to do

are _____
(ideas: blagga-bloog, grimp)

and _____ .
(ideas: biddle, froomp)

What ARE
those things?!

Is this whole book
a trick?

Can I stop reading,
please?

And now it is time to declare some new rules.

Oh, good.
I like rules.

1. Every day, everyone must eat

_____ **for breakfast.**

(ideas: ice cream, birthday cake)

What?

2. Everyone's bedtime is

_____ .

(ideas: midnight, never, outer space)

Excuse me?

3. Everyone must

_____ **ten times**

(ideas: yo-yo, walk a dog, galoomba-dance)

a day.

These can't be the rules!

And now it's time
for me to sing you
my favorite song!

I like to sing it
very _____.
(ideas: slooowly, growly, gurgly)

A song?

Do I really have to sing a—

♫ ogg
ogg ♫
♫ ogg

My face is

a _____ .

(ideas: log, toaster, pizza roll)

I like to eat _____
(ideas: watermelon, hammers, pillows)

with my _____
(ideas: dragon, goose, eyeball)

GUACAMOLE!!!

What?!

That doesn't even rhyme!

This book is ridiculous!

Can I stop reading yet?

No?!?

I have to read the rest?!?!

My secret real name is

ZAB ZAB

_____ ●

(ideas: beans, shoe, cactus)

No it isn't!

And my only friend in the whole wide world is a

_____ named

(ideas: moose, unicorn, emu)

BOO
BOO

_____ •

(ideas: burp, blip, beak)

BooBoo what?!

And also, the kid
I'm reading this book to is

THE _____est

(ideas: cool, clever, funni-)

IN THE HISTORY OF

KID EVER

THE ENTIRE _____ !

(ideas: world, universe, applesauce)

Because this kid wrote
a book that makes
grown-ups have to say
silly things!

Oh, really?

and . . .

make silly sounds like . . .

oh no oh no here it comes . . .

By now you're ready to fill in the blanks without my ideas!

GLuURR-
GA-_____!

_____

_____

_____

_____

_____ !!!!!!!!!

_____

\-

_____   _____

_____ .

HEAD!!!!!

Oh

my

goodness.

Please don't
ever
make me read
this book again!

It is completely
and utterly
preposterous!

Next time you write a book,
please please please please
please
write a serious one.

With **pictures.**

Please?
Because this is just too
ridiculous
to read.

The End

BLURP

_____!
(ideas: gack, doop, bip)

I didn't want to say that.

To the writer

Dial Books for Young Readers
An imprint of Penguin Random House LLC, New York

Visit us online at penguinrandomhouse.com

Printed in the United States of America
ISBN 9780593111017

10 9 8 7 6 5 4 3 2

Text set in Sentinel, Gotham, and Zemke Hand